PJMASKS

Mystery Mountain Adventure!

W9-BDO-118

Based on the episode "The Mountain Prisoner"

SIMON SPOTLIGHT
An imprint of Simon & Schuster Children's Publishing Division
New York   London   Toronto   New Delhi   Sydney
1230 Avenue of the Americas, New York, New York 10020
This Simon Spotlight paperback edition May 2019
This book is based on the TV series PJ MASKS © Frog Box / Entertainment One UK Limited / Walt Disney EMEA Productions Limited 2014;
Les Pyjamasques by Romuald © (2007) Gallimard Jeunesse. All Rights Reserved. This book/publication © Entertainment One UK Limited 2019.
Adapted by Lisa Lauria from the series PJ Masks
For information about special discounts for bulk purchases, please contact Simon & Schuster Special Sales at 1-866-506-1949 or business@simonandschuster.com.
Manufactured in the United States of America 0619 LAK
4 6 8 10 9 7 5 3
ISBN 978-1-5344-4393-8 (pbk)
ISBN 978-1-5344-4394-5 (eBook)

When Amaya, Connor, and Greg learn about a mystical mountain, they go straight to the library to do some research.

"I still can't believe there's a mystical mountain right in our very own city," Greg says.

Then Connor realizes that the books about the mountain are missing . . . and he spots Ninjalino footprints.

"Night Ninja!" Amaya cries. "He's planning on going back to Mystery Mountain!"

"Not if we can help it," Greg says.

The PJ Masks head to HQ. PJ Robot shows them that the Ninjalinos are reading all the books about Mystery Mountain! "Something tells me Night Ninja's up to no good," Catboy shouts. "To the Cat-Car!"

The PJ Masks go to the bench where Night Ninja and the Ninjalinos were reading the books, but they are gone! Catboy activates his Super Cat Ears and learns that the Ninjalinos have taken PJ Robot!
"They're heading for the Mountain portal!" Owlette says.

"We're coming, PJ Robot!" Gekko cries.

Gekko performs the ninja move to open the portal.

When the PJ Masks find Night Ninja, he says he won't return PJ Robot until the PJ Masks give him the Ring of Ninjability. It makes ninja powers three times stronger.

The PJ Masks want to save PJ Robot, but the ring is in a pagoda at the top of the mountain, which is filled with traps!

Night Ninja reads aloud from a book about Mystery Mountain and tells them, "Now it says here—*to open the door, solve this riddle: One by one the heroes come. But who finds the ring? Not a single one*!"

The PJ Masks arrive at the pagoda, and Gekko scans the area. "So where are these booby traps?" he asks. "I can't see any...." Just then he steps on a stone that catapults him into the air!

"Super Cat Stripes!" Catboy yells, and catches Gekko.
    Each stone on the ground of the pagoda has a monkey, a crown, or a lion. When Catboy steps on a crown stone, vines curl around his legs! Owlette and Gekko rip away the vines just in time for the PJ Masks to get to the pagoda doors.

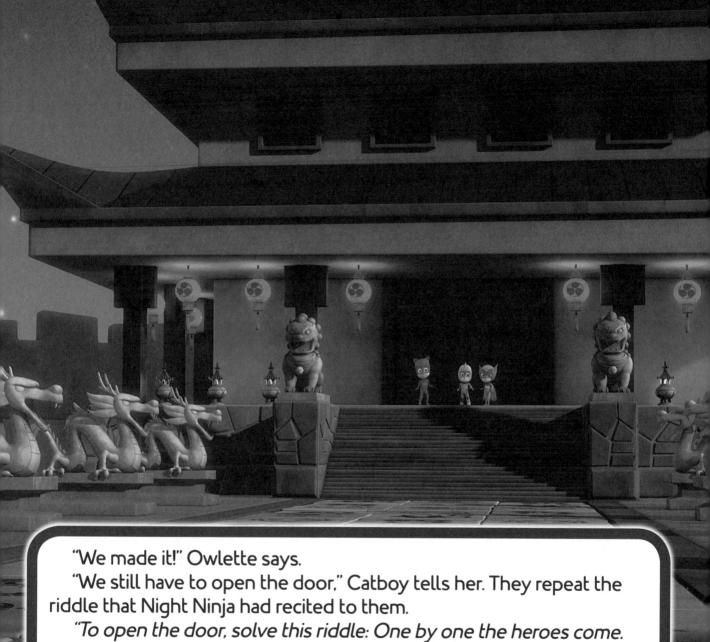

"We made it!" Owlette says.

"We still have to open the door," Catboy tells her. They repeat the riddle that Night Ninja had recited to them.

"*To open the door, solve this riddle: One by one the heroes come. But who finds the ring? Not a single one.*"

The PJ Masks still don't know what to do!

"Wait," Owlette cries out. "Who finds the ring? Not a single ONE. So let's do the opposite of 'one by one'!"

"And use our powers together!" Gekko adds.

"Let's show those doors some PJ Power," Catboy says.

"Save PJ Robot! Save PJ Robot!" the PJ Masks shout. The door slides open. Catboy grabs the Ring of Ninjability!

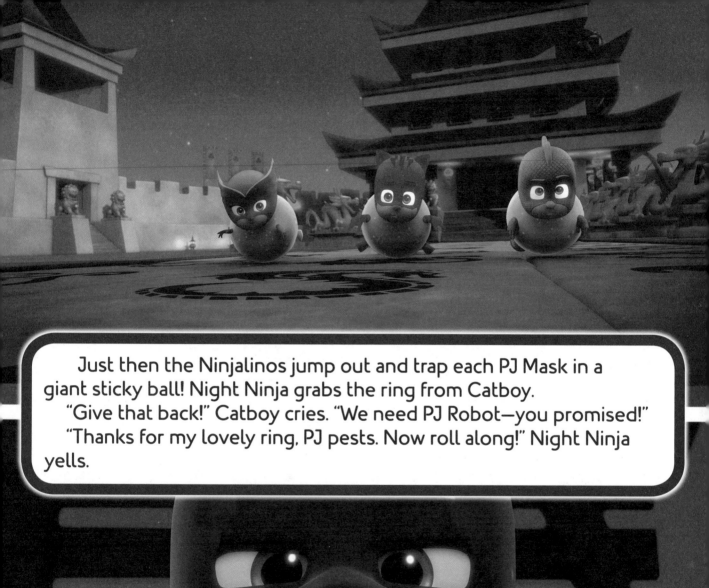

Just then the Ninjalinos jump out and trap each PJ Mask in a giant sticky ball! Night Ninja grabs the ring from Catboy.

"Give that back!" Catboy cries. "We need PJ Robot—you promised!"

"Thanks for my lovely ring, PJ pests. Now roll along!" Night Ninja yells.

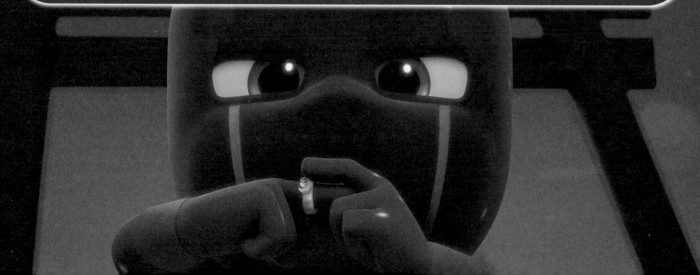

Meanwhile PJ Robot is secretly escaping from his trap. Suddenly he lands on the PJ Masks and quickly frees them.

"We just proved that when we put our powers together, we can do anything!" Catboy cheers. "I think it's time we gave those naughty ninjas a surprise!"

Night Ninja is trying to summon the powers of the ring when the PJ Masks burst through the doors.

"Now it's time to find out who's got the REAL power!" Owlette says. "Whoever gets the ring has to put their powers together, like we did!"

The PJ Masks strike a ninja pose and out-skill Night Ninja and the Ninjalinos. The ring disappears over a cliff!

"PJ Masks all shout hooray! 'Cause in the night we saved the day!" the PJ Masks cheer.